Madison & The Amazing Car

Written by Lisa Laliberte

Illustrations by Brandy Johnson

AuthorHouse™
1663 Liberty Drive
Bloomington, IN 47403
www.authorhouse.com
Phone: 833-262-8899

Because of the dynamic nature of the Internet, any web addresses or links contained in this book may have changed
since publication and may no longer be valid. The views expressed in this work are solely those of the author and do
not necessarily reflect the views of the publisher, and the publisher hereby disclaims any responsibility for them.

This book is printed on acid-free paper.

ISBN: 978-1-4343-3480-0 (sc)

Library of Congress Control Number: 2007908885

Print information available on the last page.

Published by AuthorHouse 03/05/2021

authorHOUSE®

Madison loved to travel far.

She would climb right into her Mommy's car.

Right there she would sit and imagine BIG,
thinking of places she'd never been.

Pushing every button in sight, she knew she would find the one that would give her flight.

High, high into the sky she flew, till she smiled above the earth and all she knew.

The galaxies were BIG and plenty, and yes, Madison had traveled many.

Zigging and zagging, she had found that special one.

Thrusting forward with all her might,
she zoomed right in and landed right.

Taking a deep sigh and with a big smile,
she hopped right out.

She heard some music way off and skipped on over.

"I am here, dear friends," she did cry, with arms straight out and open wide.

"Three cheers for our sweet Madison,"
was said as hugs and kisses passed on by.

Merrily they sang and danced. Tales and stories, oh, they were told. Both sides began to glow.

Time was passing into night. Suddenly Madison jumped upright.

So Madison hugged her friends super tight,
and off to her car she did race.

Frantically she looked for the button to bring her flight. When she hit the one, they all cheered in delight and ZOOM: she was out of sight.

Back to earth she came home, just in time
to hear "Time to go, Madison dear."

As she started to leap out of the car, she heard a small noise, not too far. So with a puzzled look she did find, in a seat, a friend excited to no end.

With Mommy drawing near,
the little guy began to be full of fear.

"Oh, do not worry, sweet little one.
MY mommy will not come undone."

"Oh, Mommy, take a deep breath and look. Can he stay?"

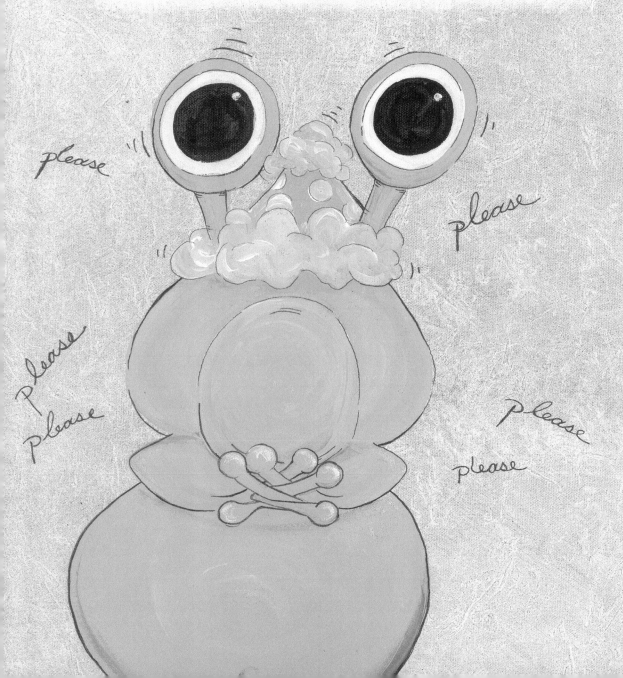

So Madison gave him a hug, and
hand in hand they did go.

"So, for now, you will rest and, Mommy, YOU ARE THE BEST!"

About the Author

Lisa R. Laliberte resides in Naples, Florida with her husband, Michael and daughter Madison.

A passion of Lisa's was to always write books; this is her first children's book.

Her daughter gave her the inspiration for this book by sharing made up stories in the car when they drove around doing errands. It was a way for them to build vocabulary and spend time with one another.

Thank you Madison for being you and as Madison would say,

Blast off with your Dreams - 7/11/07

For more, see Madison at
www.amazingadventuresofmadison.com

Printed in the United States
by Baker & Taylor Publisher Services